Groundhogs

by Cari Meister

New Hanover County Public Library
201 Chestnut Street
Wilmington, North Carolina 28401

Bullfrog Books

Ideas for Parents and Teachers

Bullfrog Books let children practice reading informational text at the earliest reading levels. Repetition, familiar words, and photo labels support early readers.

Before Reading
- Discuss the cover photo. What does it tell them?
- Look at the picture glossary together. Read and discuss the words.

Read the Book
- "Walk" through the book and look at the photos. Let the child ask questions. Point out the photo labels.
- Read the book to the child, or have him or her read independently.

After Reading
- Prompt the child to think more. Ask: Have you seen a groundhog before? What do you think it's like to wake up after hibernating all winter?

Bullfrog Books are published by Jump!
5357 Penn Avenue South
Minneapolis, MN 55419
www.jumplibrary.com

Copyright © 2015 Jump! International copyright reserved in all countries. No part of this book may be reproduced in any form without written permission from the publisher.

Library of Congress Cataloging-in-Publication Data

Meister, Cari, author.
 Groundhogs / by Cari Meister.
    pages cm. — (Bullfrog books.
My first animal library)
 Audience: Age 5.
 Audience: K to grade 3.
 Includes bibliographical references and index.
 ISBN 978-1-62031-167-7 (hardcover) —
 ISBN 978-1-62496-254-7 (ebook)
 1. Woodchuck—Juvenile literature. I. Title.
QL737.R68M45 2015
599.36'6—dc23

2014032095

Series Editor: Wendy Dieker
Series Designer: Ellen Huber
Book Designer: Michelle Sonnek
Photo Researcher: Michelle Sonnek

Photo Credits: All photos by Shutterstock except: age fotostock, 10, 18–19, 20–21, 23bl, 23br; Dreamstime, 15; Getty, 14, 22; iStock, 4, 23tl, 24; SuperStock, 3, 8; Thinkstock, 23tr.

Printed in the United States of America at Corporate Graphics in North Mankato, Minnesota.

Table of Contents

Spring Awakening	4
Parts of a Groundhog	22
Picture Glossary	23
Index	24
To Learn More	24

Spring Awakening

It is spring.
A groundhog wakes up.

He looks out of his burrow.

He is hungry.

He was hibernating for 150 days!

He has not had food.

The groundhog looks for food.

He finds grass and flowers.

His long teeth bite.
They never stop growing.

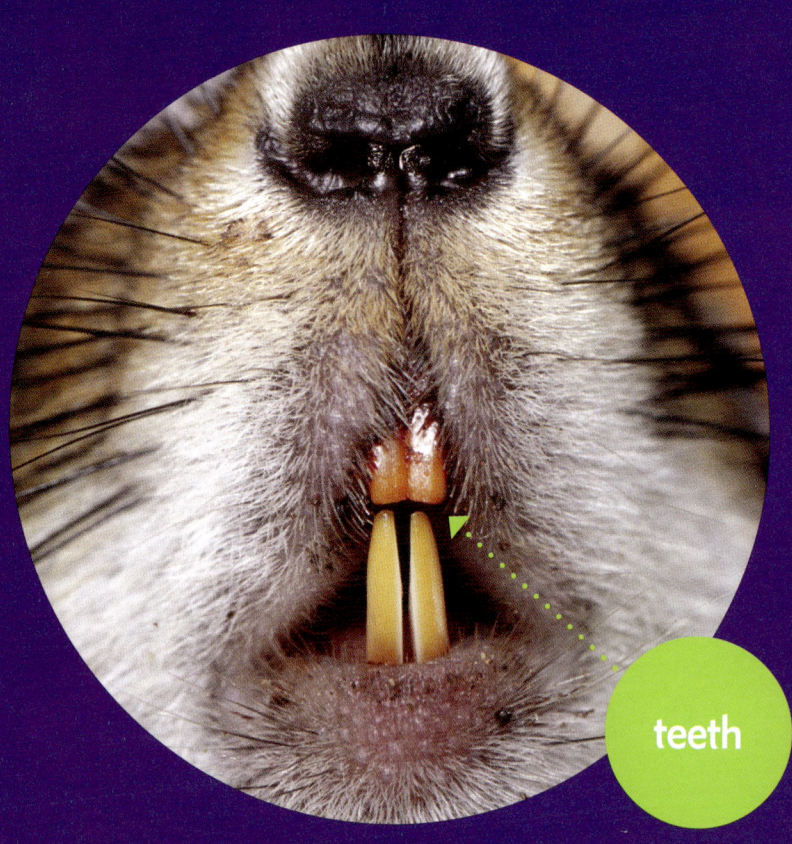

teeth

Oh no! A fox!

The fox wants to eat him!

The groundhog runs.

He climbs a tree.

He is safe.

Later, he comes down.
He looks for a female.
He sniffs.
He follows the smell.

The groundhogs find each other.

Soon she has babies.
Do you see her kits?
Hello, kits!

Parts of a Groundhog

claws
Groundhogs use these hard nails to dig.

fur
Thick fur keeps groundhogs warm.

teeth
A groundhog's incisor teeth grow its whole life.

Picture Glossary

burrow
A groundhog's underground home.

hibernating
When an animal rests or sleeps during the winter.

female
An animal that can give birth to young.

kits
Baby groundhogs.

Index

babies 20	hibernating 6
burrow 5	kits 20
female 16	smell 16
flowers 9	spring 4
food 6, 8	teeth 10
fox 12	tree 15

To Learn More

Learning more is as easy as 1, 2, 3.

1) Go to www.factsurfer.com

2) Enter "groundhogs" into the search box.

3) Click the "Surf" button to see a list of websites.

With factsurfer.com, finding more information is just a click away.